CW00493760

5

Contents

*C = copper; B = bronze.
† tpt = trumpet, cornet or flugelhorn; hn = E flat horn or French horn; LB = trombone, baritone, euphonium or tuba.

Alternative versions
Horn parts are available in both E flat and F versions.
Parts for lower-brass instruments are available in both treble (B flat) and bass clef (C) versions.

Follow the Leader

Nick Breeze

Duet # Sing Something Simple

Paul Archibald

AB 3202

Duet   The Lighthouse

Phil Croydon

Duet   Sharing

Ian Lowes

Duet   # Rhyming Couplets

David Mitcham

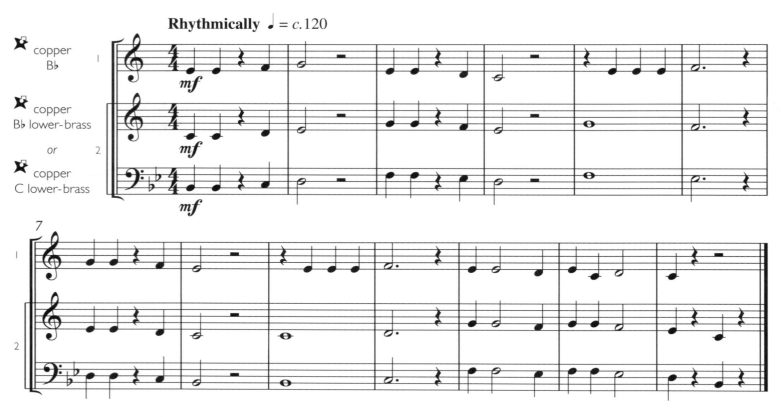

Duet   # The North Pole

Nick Breeze

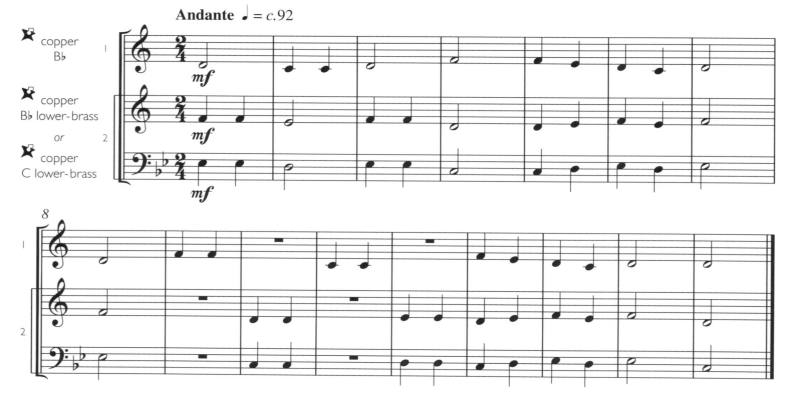

AB 3202

Duet　Double Trouble

John Miller

Trio   # Spring Surprise (i)

Philip Sparke

Trio   # Spring Surprise (ii)

Philip Sparke

6   AB 3202

A Lesson from Zia Maria

Chris Batchelor

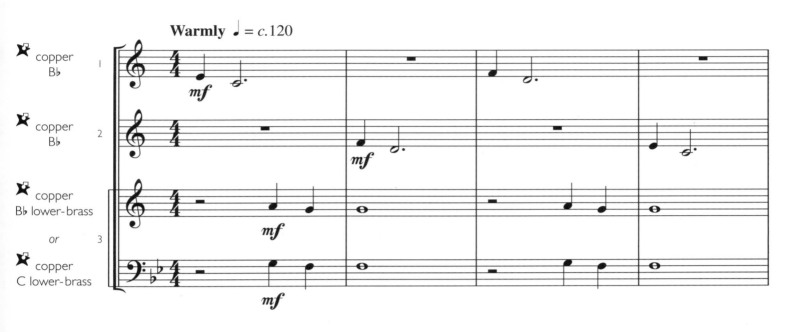

AB 3202

Trio Chorale (i)

Adrian Taylor

Trio Chorale (ii)

Adrian Taylor

AB 3202

Trio Sidesaddle

John Frith

Trio   # Jamaican Rumble

Paul Archibald

AB 3202

Quartet Cajun Cakewalk (i)

Phil Croydon

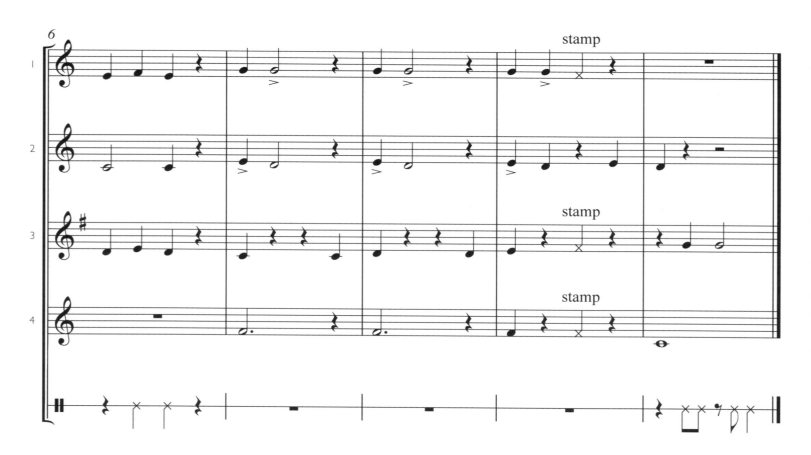

AB 3202

Quartet Cajun Cakewalk (ii)

Phil Croydon

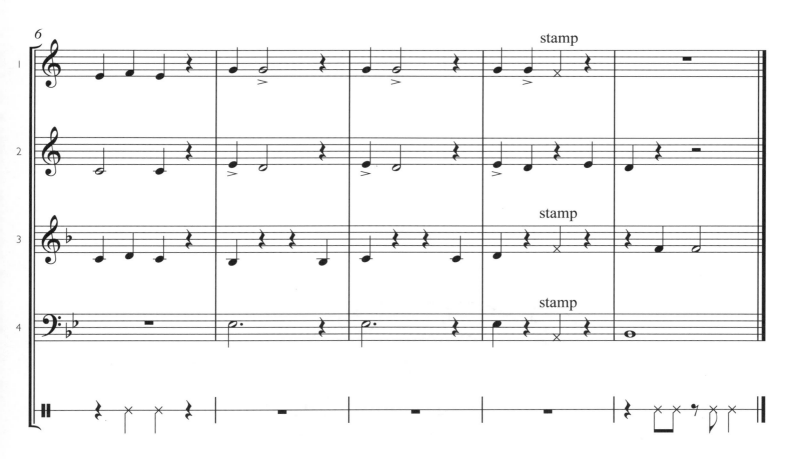

AB 3202

Quartet Across the Wide Snake River (i)

David Mitcham

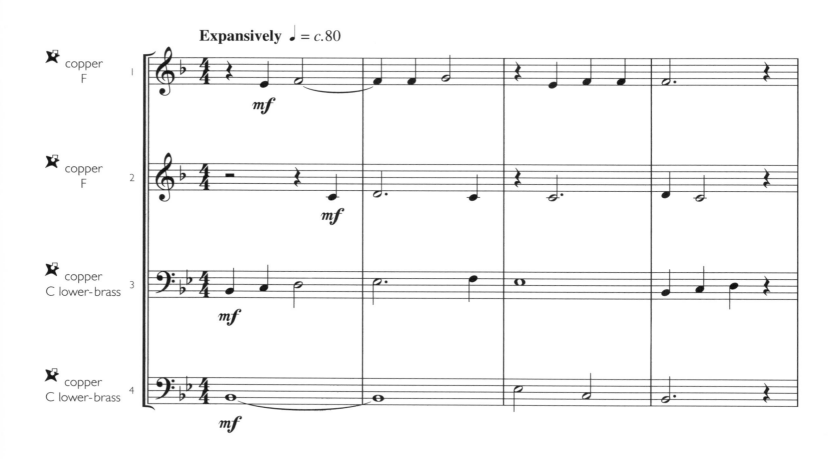

AB 3202

Quartet Across the Wide Snake River (ii)

David Mitcham

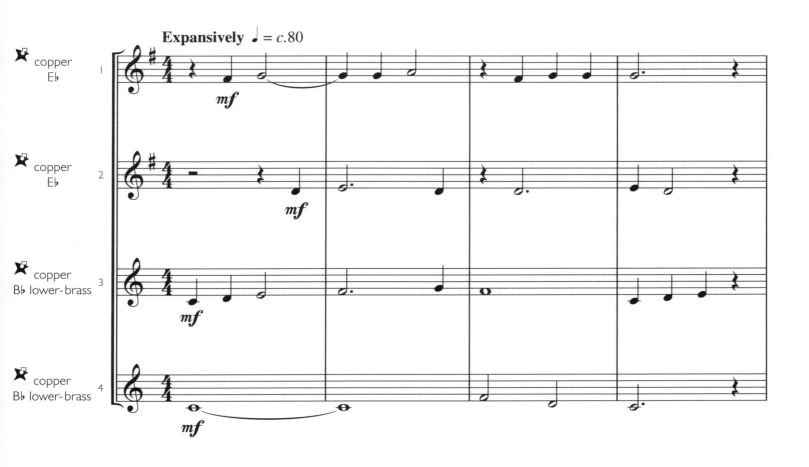

AB 3202

Quartet Blues for Four (i)

Nick Breeze

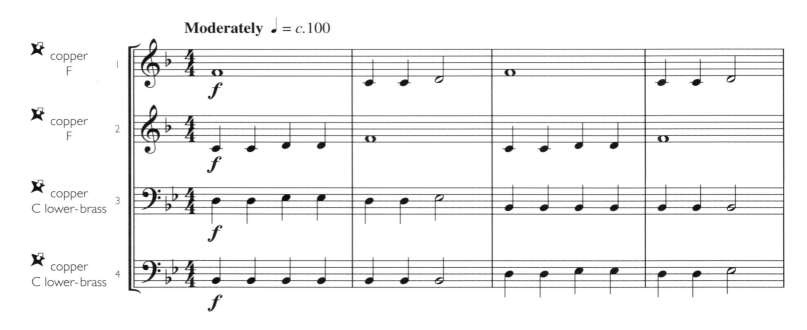

AB 3202

Quartet Blues for Four (ii)

Nick Breeze

Quartet The Donkey's Parade (i)

Adrian Taylor

AB 3202

Quartet The Donkey's Parade (ii)

Adrian Taylor

AB 3202